Published in 2009 by Windmill Books, LLC
303 Park Avenue South, Suite # 1280, New York, NY 10010-3657

Text copyright © 2009 Hilary Robinson
Illustrations copyright © 2009 Mike Gordon
Additional illustration work by Carl Gordon

Publisher Cataloging Data

Robinson, Hilary, 1962-
        A croc shock! / by Hilary Robinson ; illustrated by Mike Gordon.
                p.   cm. – (Get set readers)
        Summary: Simple rhyming text and colorful illustrations tell about Jake seeing what he thinks is a crocodile in the fishing lake.
        ISBN 978-1-60754-265-0
        1. Fishing—Juvenile fiction   2. Crocodiles—Juvenile fiction
[1. Fishing—Fiction   2. Crocodiles—Fiction   3. Stories in rhyme]
I. Gordon, Mike   II. Title   III. Series
        [E]—dc22

Manufactured in the United States of America

A Croc Shock!

by Hilary Robinson

illustrated by Mike Gordon

alphabet SOUP

an imprint of

WINDMILL BOOKS
New York

When Jake took his net...

...to fish by the rock

he saw what he thought...

...was the eye of a croc!

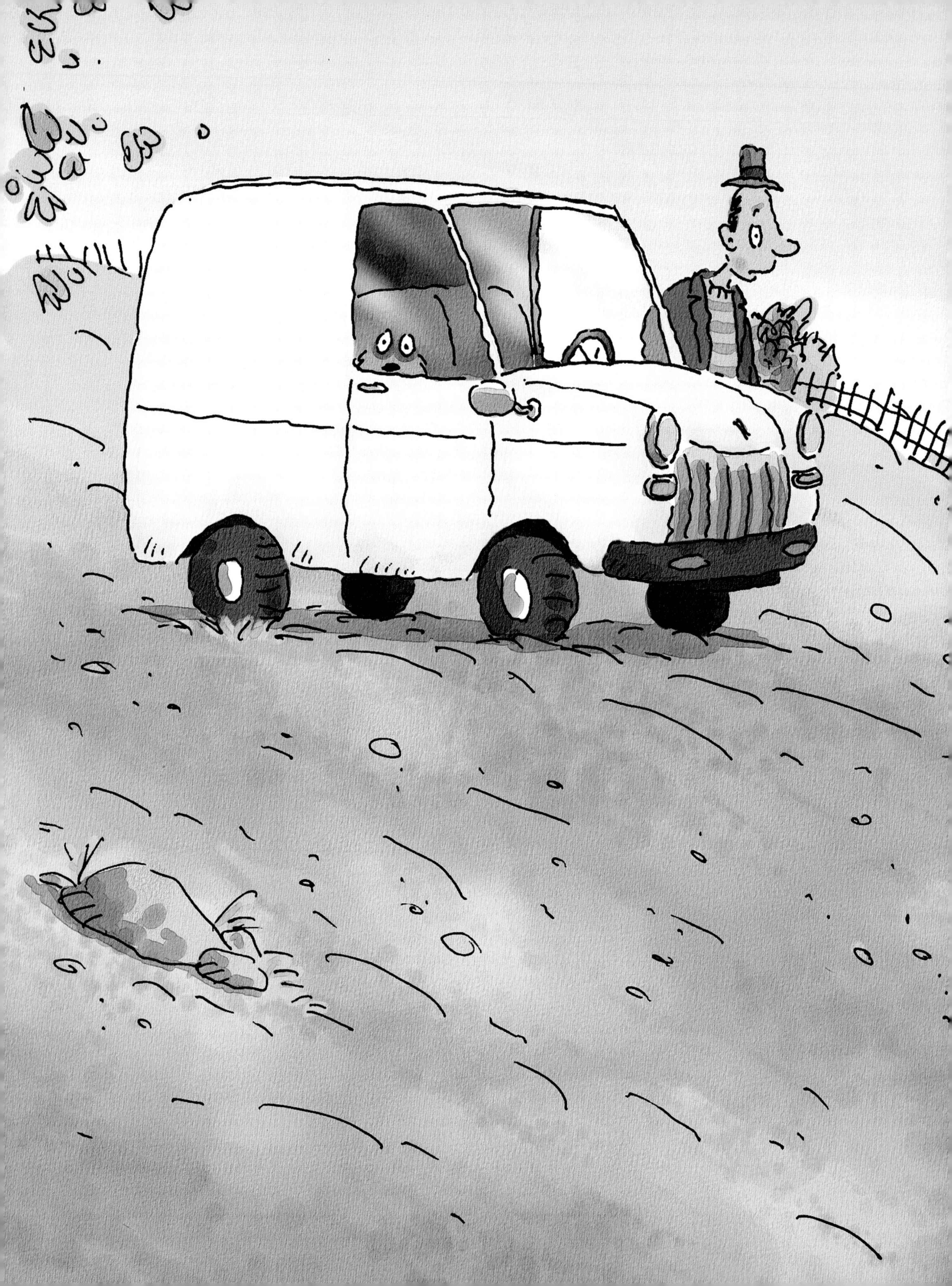

"A croc by the rock!"
Jake called to the man...

...who let his dog out

from the back of a van.

The dog stretched his paws

then raced around
the rock...

...then jumped in the lake

to hunt for the croc!

He dipped and he dived

as the kids rushed to take...

...some photographs of

the croc in the lake.

Then everyone cheered

as the dog showed to all...

...that the crocodile's eye

was only a ball!

But later that day

Jake fished on the rock...

...and found in his net...

...a tooth from a croc!

For more great fiction and nonfiction, go to www.windmillbks.com.